Dil in Transit

Flights, Feelings & Fate
A Desi Romcom

Simran Bhandari

ISBN: **978-93-344-4215-1**
First Published in India, 2025

Table of Content

The Wrong Flight

If my life were a rom-com, the airport announcement would've said, "Gate change for destiny." Instead, it just said, "Final boarding call for Flight 6E-245 to Dharamshala."

And like the overworked, overtired, over-caffeinated idiot that I am, I ran. Dragging my laptop bag, camera pouch, and dignity across Terminal 2, I sprinted like a woman possessed because I was. Possessed by the fear of losing yet another client over something as stupid as being late.

The Goa event was my biggest campaign of the quarter. Luxury travel brand, influencer tie-ups, beachfront backdrop everything I'd worked for. And now, here I was, running through a crowd of selfie-stick-wielding tourists, praying to every god, spirit, and airport deity I could think of available in Economy class.

"Ma'am, boarding pass?" the flight attendant asked, giving me that polite-but-judgy Indigo smile. I handed it over, panting. She scanned it, smiled wider, and waved me through.

Success.

I slid into my window seat, hair frizzy, blazer wrinkled, lungs in protest. The man next to me was already asleep, headphones on, legs spread, one of those people who behave like Economy is their ancestral property.

As the plane took off, I tried to calm my pulse.
Just Goa. Just a work trip. Just another flight.

Except... thirty minutes later, when the announcement came... "Cabin crew, please prepare for descent into Dharamshala"
I realized my life was about to take a U-turn. Literally.

Cue existential silence.

I checked my boarding pass. Twice. Then thrice. Seat 17A. Flight 6E-245. It was right there except the destination was not. Apparently, I radiate such chaotic confidence that even the scanner didn't dare disagree.

Goa. Dharamshala.
How the hell does one even confuse sea breeze with pine trees?

My phone had no signal. The passenger beside me stirred, removed his headphones, and looked right at me with the world's most annoyingly calm smile.

"First time?" he asked.

"What?"

"Getting on the wrong flight." He grinned. "Happens more than you'd think. I once boarded a flight to Ranchi instead of Raipur. Ended up having the best biryani of my life, though."

I blinked at him. "I'm supposed to be in Goa. I have a client presentation in six hours." He tilted his head, pretending to think. "Well, unless your client's a monk, you're in trouble."

I glared. "Do you ever stop talking?"

"Not when I'm sitting next to a woman having a full-blown identity crisis mid-air," he said, still grinning. "I'm Arjun, by the way. Arjun Mehta."

I didn't reply. I was too busy recalculating my entire existence.

When we landed, the view outside looked like God had turned on an HD filter: misty hills, winding roads, and air so clean it felt personal. And I hated it. Because every breathtaking view was one missed meeting, one furious client, one ruined plan.

While the other passengers gathered their luggage, I stood there, frozen in disbelief, until a flight attendant gently asked, “Ma’am, are you waiting for someone?”
“Yes,” I said, deadpan. “Common sense. I missed this flight too.”

Outside the tiny Gaggal airport, it started to drizzle, not the cinematic type, but the “let’s ruin your outfit and your mood” kind. I called my assistant, Priya, but of course there was no network. Because the Himalayas apparently believe in emotional detox.

“Need a cab?”
The same man.. Arjun.. stood beside me, holding a coffee cup and an expression that screamed amused spectator.

“No, thanks. I’m trying to manifest a private jet,” I said, shivering.

He laughed. “Manifestation’s great and all, but they just canceled the return flights. Landslides on the route. You’ll have to drive down to Chandigarh at least.”

My stomach dropped. “You’re kidding.”

He sipped his coffee like a man who thrived on other people’s misfortunes. “Nope. Already booked a cab. Want to split?”

I opened my mouth to refuse. But then, the universe.. my new unpaid intern.. decided to mess with me further.

The rain intensified. My phone died. And his driver showed up holding a placard that said “Mr. Mehta + Guest.” “I’m not your guest,” I said. He shrugged. “Fine. Be my co-passenger. Unless you prefer meditating here till the network returns.”

I exhaled, defeated. “One ride. That’s it.”

He grinned, like he’d just won something. “Relax, Miss Goa-Not-Goa. It’s just a lift, not a proposal.”

The cab smelled like wet seats and bad decisions. Arjun sat with his elbow out the window, humming to some indie track while I typed aggressively on my dead phone. He caught me glancing. “You know, you look like someone who has a five-year plan for everything, except getting lost.”

“I don’t get lost,” I muttered. “I reroute.”
“Reroute,” he repeated, chuckling. “Cute word for denial.”

I turned to the window, counting to ten. He was insufferable. The man who’d flirt with chaos and call it adventure.

And yet, there was something in his ease, the way he laughed, the way he made even being stranded feel like a scene, that kind of got under my skin. He wasn't trying to impress anyone. He was just... alive.

Alive enough to make even the road seem awake. We drove through hills wrapped in mist, the world narrowing to damp air and the hum of the tires. Every few turns, a tea stall appeared like a checkpoint for patience. At one of them, Arjun insisted we stop. A sleepy man handed us paper cups of chai so sweet it could melt heartbreak.

Arjun lifted his cup toward me. "To missed flights."
I rolled my eyes. "You make it sound romantic."
"Everything is romantic if you're stuck long enough to notice," he said, sipping.

A group of kids ran past, chasing a plastic bottle as if it were a football. A cow blocked the narrow road, refusing to move until Arjun got out and negotiated like a diplomat. I watched him gesture, laugh, and surrender. When he returned, hair wet and face bright, I realised he looked like freedom. Careless. Infuriating. Magnetic.

By the time we got back on the road, the rain had softened into mist. An hour later, we pulled up at a dhaba perched on the edge of a valley, clouds grazing the tin roof. I sat down reluctantly, watching him order like a local: parathas, butter, chai, the full movie-scene experience.

"You don't eat?" he asked.

"I do. Just not food that looks like it was fried in nostalgia."

He laughed so hard he almost spilled the chai. "You're impossible."

"And you're..."

"Charming?"

"...loud."

We ate in silence after that. Well, mostly silence. He hummed a Kishore Kumar song under his breath while I tried to remember why I ever thought I liked traveling.

When we left the dhaba, a group of backpackers waved at us. One of them, a vlogger, asked if he could take a quick video. "Sure," Arjun said before I could object. The vlogger pointed his camera and said, "Couple goals in the Himalayas!" I froze. "We're not..." But Arjun just leaned in, smiled at the camera, and said, "Wrong flight, right company." And just like that, the rain-soaked, laughter-filled chaos of our clip took over the internet overnight.

By the time we hit the mountain curves, the rain had slowed into a lazy drizzle that looks romantic only in other people's reels. Inside our cab, silence had started to stretch like overchewed gum.

his head tilted back, eyes closed, tapping his on his thigh to some rhythm only he could hear. I …hed him for a second, against my better judgment. He looked annoyingly peaceful, like people who claim meditation fixed their anxiety when really, they just have good genetics.

"Do you ever take anything seriously?" I finally asked.

He opened one eye. "Depends. Is this a trick question?"

"I'm just saying," I continued, "you're stuck in a cab with a stranger, in the middle of nowhere, and you're..."

"...enjoying it?" he interrupted. "Yeah, guilty as charged."

I sighed. "You're impossible."

"See, you keep saying that, but your tone is starting to sound impressed."

I looked away, refusing to give him that satisfaction. The man had a PhD in irritation and an honorary degree in timing.

Somewhere between rain puddles and roadside temples, we started talking. Against my will. He told me he used to work in finance, "until I realized I'd rather be broke and breathing than rich and dying slowly in a cubicle." Now he runs a small eco-travel startup with his college friends: road trips, sustainable stays, mountains, stories. Basically, everything I considered a logistical nightmare.

When I asked him what made him quit his "respectable job," he shrugged and said, "I didn't quit. I just stopped pretending spreadsheets could save my soul."
I didn't know whether to laugh or roll my eyes. So I did both.

He asked me what I did. "Marketing strategist," I said. "So basically, you convince people they need what they don't," he teased.
"And you convince people they're saving the planet by glamping," I shot back.
He grinned. "Touché."

Hours later, as the sun melted behind the hills, our cab stopped at a small roadside guesthouse as the driver refused to continue in the dark. "Too risky, madam. Landslides," he said.

I checked my watch - 8:47 p.m.
Goa presentation: canceled.
My boss: probably plotting my corporate funeral.
My life: a meme.

The owner of the guesthouse gave us one room. One. Apparently, they were overbooked thanks to "offbeat travel influencers."

Arjun looked at me, clearly enjoying the cosmic joke. "Relax," he said. "I'll sleep on the floor. I've done worse. Once spent a night in a broken tent during a hailstorm."

"Congratulations," I muttered. "Do you want a medal or a mosquito net?"

He chuckled, spreading his jacket on the floor. I climbed onto the creaky bed, pulled the blanket, and faced the wall. For a while, all I could hear was the soft hum of rain on the roof and him softly strumming a tune on his phone. It was maddeningly gentle.

"Can you not?" I said.
"Music calms me," he replied.
"It annoys me."
"Exactly why you need it."

I turned to glare, but his eyes were closed, head leaning against the wall, a faint smile playing on his lips, like he'd perfected the art of being unbothered. For a fleeting second, I envied it.

At some point, I fell asleep. When I woke up, the rain had stopped. The early light slanted through the curtains, painting everything gold. Arjun was gone.

His jacket lay folded neatly on the chair, and next to it, a note, scrawled on a napkin:

———

"Caught an early cab. Thanks for the unplanned detour. You should try getting lost more often. — A."

———

I stared at it longer than I should've. Outside, the morning fog made the hills shimmer, quiet, unapologetic, and full of life. I stepped out for air, phone finally catching signal. Ten missed calls from my boss. A dozen from Priya. And one notification that made me freeze.
@MapsAndMishaps *tagged you in a reel.*
I opened it.

There we were, me rain-soaked and rolling my eyes, while Arjun laughed beside me, speaking into the camera:
"Wrong flight, right company."
The caption read:
When the universe plays travel agent.

In twelve hours, it had a hundred thousand views. Hundreds of comments:

"These two are totally dating."
"Find someone who looks at you like he does."
"Is this a movie or real life?"

I closed the app, my stomach sinking. I didn't know whether to laugh, cry, or throw my phone into the valley. All I knew was, the algorithm had just shipped me with a stranger. And I had a feeling... this wouldn't be the last time our paths crossed.

Of Tea, Tunes, and Tempers

I've always believed the universe has a sense of humor.
The problem is I'm usually the punchline.

After Arjun left that morning, I convinced myself the detour was over. I'd book the next flight to Mumbai, face my boss's wrath, apologize to the client, and bury this entire Dharamshala episode under the folder titled "Things We Don't Talk About After Wine."

Except, when I reached the airport, the receptionist gave me the kind of smile people reserve for bad news.
"Ma'am, all flights are canceled again. Weather warning."

Of course.
Of course the Himalayas wanted a sequel.

I walked out to the same drizzle, same empty road, same realization: I was stranded. That's when a familiar voice called out, "Miss Goa-Not-Goa! The mountain gods clearly missed you."

Arjun stood there with the same messy hair, same smug grin, holding two cups of steaming tea like a reward I hadn't earned.
"Don't tell me you're stuck too," I said.

He shrugged. "Nah. I extended my stay. Nature's better company than clients."

I took the cup anyway. Warm, sugary, and annoyingly comforting. He tilted his head, studying me. "You know, most people would take this as a sign."
"Of what?"
"That maybe they're supposed to slow down."

"I don't do signs," I said, sipping my tea. "I do schedules."

He laughed softly, like slipped under your skin before you could block it.

We found a shared cab heading toward a small village en route to Chandigarh, the only route open that day.
The car was old, smelled faintly of rain and eucalyptus, and had a driver who looked like he'd seen too many tourists cry over network loss.

Arjun played some random Hindi playlist. Kishore Kumar, Prateek Kuhad, Lucky Ali the chaotic trinity of heartbreak and wanderlust. He hummed along. Loudly. Off-key.

I tried to answer emails on my phone, but every few seconds he'd say something ridiculous like,
"Do you think clouds gossip about us?"
or

"If you had to marry one song, which one would it be?"

"None," I said. "Songs fade."
"Harsh," he replied. "You must be fun at parties."

"I am. Just not the kind you'd get invited to."

He chuckled, glancing at me. "You know, you keep saying you hate chaos, but you talk to it like an old friend."

By lunchtime, we'd stopped at a roadside shack. The signboard read Tea, Tunes & Tempers, no kidding.
The owner, a sweet old lady named Kammo, made the best ginger chai I'd ever had. Arjun helped her fix the Bluetooth speaker. In five minutes, she was blasting Ajeeb Dastan Hai Yeh and calling him "beta."

I watched him from a corner table, trying to decode his brand of ease. He made small talk with everyone with the driver, the local kid selling keychains, even the dog sleeping under the bench. There was something infuriatingly magnetic about how present he was. Like he didn't need to be anywhere else, didn't need to prove anything. Meanwhile, I was half-listening, half-calculating how many hours it would take to get back to Mumbai if I left tonight.

"You ever get tired of being perfect?" he asked suddenly, sitting across from me.

I blinked. "Excuse me?"

He smiled. "You have this... everything-in-control energy. Does it ever exhaust you?"

I wanted to deny it, but his tone, curious rather than mocking, caught me off guard. So I said quietly, "Control is about survival not perfection."

He nodded, eyes softening. "Same reason I joke all the time. Survival. Except mine comes with bad puns and worse decisions."

For a moment, the world shrank. There was no rain, no road, just two strangers sitting across a wooden table, sharing the kind of honesty people usually hide behind humor.

Later, as dusk fell, Kammo lit candles around the shack. Power cut. Arjun found a guitar lying around, because of course he did, and started strumming something raw and unpolished.

"Please tell me you're not about to sing," I groaned.
"Please tell me you're not about to complain."
He smirked, continued anyway.

It wasn't perfect, it wasn't even in tune. But there was something about it: the simplicity, the ease, the way the song seemed to melt into the rain outside.

He sang softly,

"Kuch safar, manzilon se zyada khoobsurat hote hain..."
Some journeys are more beautiful than their destinations.

And for reasons I couldn't name, I couldn't look away.

That night, we stayed at a tiny homestay nearby, a room with mismatched furniture, peeling paint, and a quiet that forced you to face yourself. He sat on the balcony, nursing tea. I joined him, wrapped in a blanket.

"Ever regret leaving finance?" I asked.
"Every time I check my bank balance," he said, smiling. "But then I remember what Mondays used to feel like and I shut up."

He looked at me then, really looked.
"What about you? Ever regret playing it safe?"

The question hit harder than expected. I wanted to say no. That I loved my career, my structure, my color-coded Google Calendar. But all I could manage was, "Sometimes."

"Sometimes," he repeated softly, like he was saving the word for later.

We talked until the sky turned velvet, about exes who broke us, jobs that defined us, and the strange pull of wanting more. There was laughter. There were long pauses. There were almosts. At one point, he told me about a song he never finished writing. At another, I told him about a person I never finished loving. The air between us grew heavy, that slow, electric tension that comes when two people realize they've accidentally stepped into something that could matter.

When the clock struck two, I stood up abruptly. "I should sleep. Early start tomorrow."
He nodded, as if he already knew I was running.

I left at dawn. Quietly. No goodbye note, no chai, no sign that I had ever been there. My cab rattled down the hill road while the village was still asleep. As I looked back, I saw the faint outline of the homestay balcony and maybe, just maybe, a figure standing there, watching.

I didn't wave. I didn't stop. Because that's what I do best: leave before it gets real. But halfway through the drive, my phone buzzed. Unknown number. One message. "You forgot your scarf. I'll keep it till the next wrong flight."

I smiled despite myself. Maybe the universe wasn't done with its sense of humor yet.

Back to the Grind

Mumbai doesn't wait for anyone. Not even a woman who just accidentally fell for a stranger on a mountain.

By the time my cab crossed the Bandra flyover, the rain had become the city's favorite mood swing, somewhere between drizzle and chaos. Skyscrapers blinked like overworked insomniacs. Billboards screamed SALE! and COMING SOON! and BE MORE PRODUCTIVE! as if the city had a personal vendetta against rest. I reached my apartment, dropped my suitcase, and fell onto the couch. For the first time in days, the silence was heavy, that makes you scroll through your phone just to fill the air with noise.

I opened Instagram.
Bad idea.

The reel.
Still there.
Still viral.

Wrong flight, right company. A million views. A thousand comments. A hundred reposts. People had shipped us harder than I shipped my own deadlines.
Couple edits. Fan captions. One user even wrote, "Petition to make them a series."

I wanted to scream.
Or laugh.
Or maybe just admit that I'd watched it more times than I should have.

The next morning, I was back at the office with hair tied, heels on, pretending like my emotional mess had an on/off switch.
"Morning, boss," my assistant Priya chirped, handing me coffee.
"Morning," I said, taking a sip. "How bad's the damage?"
"Client was furious. I told them you were stuck in unpredictable weather."
"Technically true."
"They think you meant the Goa thunderstorm, not the mountain monsoon."
I groaned. "Right. Remind me to buy you something nice."
"You already owe me therapy money," she said, deadpan.

By noon, I'd drowned myself in emails, campaign reports, and the one thing that never judged me, Google Sheets. Every few minutes, though, my brain betrayed me with flashes of Arjun's grin, his stupid "clouds gossip" line, that unfinished song humming in the background of my thoughts. It wasn't love. It was just memory residue. (At least that's what I told myself. Repeatedly. Like a chant.)

When I finally called Aisha that evening, she answered on the second ring, voice calm like she'd been expecting it.
"So," she said. "Did you find enlightenment or at least a cute monk in the mountains?"
"I found a disaster with dimples," I muttered.
She gasped theatrically. "Tell me everything."

I did. Every ridiculous, rain-soaked, chai-filled moment. The wrong flight, the dhaba, the viral reel, the scarf I forgot. When I finished, she was quiet for a second. Then she said, in her annoyingly therapist tone,
"Sounds like you met someone who reminded you that control isn't peace."
"Please don't psychoanalyze me like I'm one of your clients," I said, lying on my bed, staring at the ceiling.
"Then let me be your friend," she replied. "And as your friend.. he'll be back."
I scoffed. "You think the universe has time for romantic reruns?"
"Naina," she said patiently, "the universe loves reruns. That's why exes exist."
I laughed despite myself. "I'm not waiting."
"Of course not," she said lightly. "But I didn't say you had to wait. I said he'll come back."

Her voice lingered in my head long after the call ended. He'll be back. Right. And maybe I'll start believing in astrology while I'm at it.

Two weeks passed. Life, as it does, returned to its regularly scheduled programming: meetings, caffeine, deadlines, and pretending your heart didn't stutter every time a mountain ad showed up on your feed. But apparently, the algorithm was determined to ruin me. Because every time I opened Instagram, there he was.
Arjun Mehta.
Sitting on some cliff with a guitar, captioning reels with lines like,
"Don't chase sunsets. Let them find you."

Ugh.
Men with philosophy should be a red flag.

I told myself it didn't matter. That what happened in Dharamshala was a fluke. People meet, people vanish, people forget. That's how grown-up life works... right?

And then Monday arrived with its favorite twist: an emergency meeting. Our CEO, Mr. Chatterjee, stood in the boardroom like he was about to deliver a sermon. "Team, we've landed a massive new client, an eco-travel startup based out of Delhi. Young, viral, growing fast. We'll be handling their brand campaign for India launch."

I nodded absently, half-listening while scrolling through notes. Until Priya nudged me. Hard.

“Ma’am,” she whispered. “Look at the name.”

I looked at the deck on screen.

Client: Horizon Trails (Founder: Arjun Mehta).

The universe didn’t just play reruns, it wrote them in bold font and PowerPoint transitions.

I tried to keep a neutral expression, but my brain short-circuited. Mr. Chatterjee clapped. “Naina, you’ll be leading this campaign. The client requested someone with your travel branding experience. First meeting’s tomorrow.”

Requested.

Requested.

I wanted to protest. To say no. To claim sudden amnesia or dengue. Anything. But my mouth betrayed me. “Of course, sir.”

As soon as the meeting ended, Priya cornered me near the coffee machine.

“Wait, that Arjun?” she whispered.

“Apparently.”

“The one from the viral reel?”

“Can you not say that so loudly?”

She grinned. “Universe’s PR team is working overtime for you, ma’am.”

I groaned. “I swear, if he even mentions that reel...”

“...you’ll what? Fall for him again?”

I threw a sugar sachet at her. She ducked, laughing.

That night, sleep mocked me. I kept replaying everything, the cab ride, the tea, that half-finished song. And that stupid napkin note I still hadn't thrown away. He'll be back, Aisha had said. I hated when she was right.

Next morning, 11 a.m. sharp, I entered the client meeting room at The Leela. Crisp blazer, neutral lipstick, presentation ready. I was the picture of professionalism. On the inside, though? A controlled meltdown. Then he walked in. Same messy hair. Same smile that could melt traffic. But now.. clean shirt, confidence, and an energy that said I know exactly what I'm doing.

"Ms. Khanna," he greeted, extending his hand like we hadn't shared rain, banter, and emotional intimacy in a single road trip.
"Mr. Mehta," I said coolly, shaking it.
"Didn't think we'd meet this soon," he said, eyes twinkling.
"I didn't either. Next time, I'll double-check my flight."
He chuckled, leaning back in his chair. "Maybe not. The wrong ones seem to work out better for us."

The meeting began. Half my brain focused on branding strategy; the other half tried not to notice how he looked when he was serious, sleeves rolled up, explaining sustainability metrics like it was poetry. He spoke about eco-travel, community tourism, and connecting people to nature. I added insights, data points, and ways to position it digitally. To everyone else, it looked like synergy. To me, it felt like déjà vu with a corporate twist.

When the presentation ended, our teams mingled over coffee. Arjun came up to me, holding two cups.
"Peace offering," he said.
"I'm not at war."
"Then why are you glaring at the cappuccino?"
I sighed. "You're my client now. Let's keep this professional."

He smiled infuriatingly calm and confidently.
"Sure, Ms. Khanna. But just for the record, the universe clearly didn't get that memo."

Later that night, I texted Aisha: You were right. He's back. Her reply came in seconds. I always am. Don't screw it up this time. I didn't reply. Because I wasn't sure whether this time was fate... or just another detour waiting to happen.

Hello Again, Stranger

There are two kinds of reunions in life. The first: the "oh-my-god-it's-been-forever" kind that smells like nostalgia and bad coffee. The second: the "dear-god-why-now" kind that smells like destiny having a nervous breakdown. Mine was the second one.

Three days after that meeting, our official "campaign kickoff" began. The brand Horizon Trails was launching a 3-week all-India campaign to promote sustainable travel. The plan? A team of creators, marketers, and videographers traveling through six states, shooting content for social media and brand ads. The brief sounded exciting. The reality? I was going to be stuck with him.
Arjun Mehta.
The man who thought chaos was a personality trait.

I met the team at Mumbai Airport (irony, my old enemy). I was there an hour early, triple-checked itineraries, call sheets, and budgets.
The man himself arrived thirty minutes late with sunglasses on, duffel bag, and that "rules are just polite suggestions" smile.

"Good morning, Ms. Khanna," he said, walking over like this was a movie trailer and he'd just entered in slow motion.

"You're late," I replied.
"You're early. Balance restored."

I rolled my eyes. "We have twenty-one days together. Let's not start with sarcasm."
He grinned. "That's like asking the Himalayas not to snow."

The team assembled: our videographer couple, a social media intern named Rhea, and my assistant Priya. Arjun briefed them while I updated our client sheets. But every few minutes, he'd glance at me with that faint smirk, the one that said I remember everything, even the things you pretend not to.

When our flight took off, he ended up next to me again. Of course.
"Déjà vu?" he whispered.
"Tragedy," I muttered.
He laughed under his breath. "You know, you're fun when you're annoyed."
"And you're tolerable when you're quiet."
"Which is never," he said, leaning back with that impossible calm.

Our first stop was Jaipur. Golden light, pink walls, chaos in HD. Arjun's idea was to film "authentic moments" with locals, markets, chai stalls, the real India. My idea was to follow the storyboard and not get sued for trespassing.

"Plans kill magic," he said when I asked for the shot list.
"Magic doesn't pay invoices," I replied.

Still, somewhere between haggling with shopkeepers and chasing light for reels, something started to shift.
The banter got easier. The silences got shorter.
We still argued constantly but it wasn't hostile anymore. It was... spark.

By the third day, our car rides had turned into unspoken therapy sessions. He played songs; I pretended to hate them. He teased; I retorted. He stole my coffee; I pretended not to notice when he refilled it before handing it back.

There was one particular drive golden hour stretching over the Aravallis, wind messy in my hair where he caught me smiling at nothing.

"What?" he asked.
"Nothing."
"You were smiling."
"People do that sometimes."
"Not you. You usually smirk or glare."
I turned away. "You observe too much."
"That's because you hide too well."

The words hung in the air, soft but too honest. So I changed the topic.

That night, we checked into a boutique hotel in Pushkar. The staff thought we were a couple (again, thank you universe). When the receptionist said, "Sir, should I bring dinner for two?" Arjun didn't even blink. "Yes, please. Candlelight if possible."
I glared.
He winked.

Dinner turned into drinks on the rooftop. The rest of the team had gone to sleep. The city lights shimmered below us; somewhere in the distance, temple bells echoed. He looked different in that light, softer somehow, quieter too. "Do you ever stop performing?" I asked.
He chuckled. "You think this is a performance?"
"I think this is defense."

He looked at me then, and the playful tone dropped.
"You sound like someone who's seen too many people hide behind jokes," he said.
"I sound like someone who knows what it's like to lose control," I replied.
Silence. Long. Heavy. Electric. Then he smiled gently.
"Maybe that's why we work. You anchor. I drift."

I wanted to say something. Anything. But words felt dangerous. So I just said, "We don't work. We collaborate."

He laughed softly. "Sure, Ms. Khanna. Keep telling yourself that."

The next morning, Arjun was already downstairs when I came down for breakfast. I saw him, hair damp, guitar slung on his back like a prop destiny insisted on.

"Ready?" he asked.

"For work," I said pointedly.

He grinned. "That's what I meant. Mostly."

After a few days hopping through Rajasthan, Jaipur, Pushkar, and a blur of dusty towns, we made our way north. Next leg, Delhi to Rishikesh, five hours of traffic, music, and passive-aggressive playlist wars.

The Road to Rishikesh

He insisted on driving. I insisted on surviving. Within ten minutes, he'd missed an exit, waved at a cow, and started humming something that didn't even have lyrics.

"Do you ever stay quiet?" I asked.

"Do you ever relax?" he countered.

"Not when I'm trapped in a moving death wish."

"See? Drama. You'd do great in theatre."

He was impossible. And somehow... endearing.

When the traffic stalled near Gurugram, we rolled the windows down. The air was heavy with dust, roadside food, and conversations that should've been left unsaid. He tapped the steering wheel. "Tell me one thing about you that isn't on your résumé."

I hesitated. "I cry during ads. Even the detergent ones."

He smiled. "Figures. You sell emotions for a living."

"Your turn," I said.

"I once proposed a girl in 11th grade with a PowerPoint."

I blinked. "Please tell me you're lying."

"Slide 1: 'Reasons you should say yes.' She said no before Slide 2."

I laughed. I actually laughed loud, that made him glance over like he'd just won something.

Rishikesh

By the time we reached, the sun was dipping behind the hills, painting the Ganga gold. The campaign shoot went smoother than I expected. Locals, laughter, and drone shots that made everything look more cinematic than real life. Between setups, he kept handing out tea, fixing props, making everyone laugh.

He wasn't trying to impress, he was just there. Fully present, maddeningly genuine.

Later, when the team went to explore the market, we stayed back on the suspension bridge, wind in our hair and city

lights flickering below. He leaned on the railing, eyes on the river. "You ever wonder what it's like to stop running?"
I looked at him. "You mean... stay still?"
He nodded.
"I wouldn't know how," I said softly.
He glanced sideways. "Maybe that's your next campaign... learning stillness."
I smirked. "And what's yours?"
He shrugged. "Learning roots."

The silence that followed wasn't awkward. It was full.
Like both of us knew we were standing at the edge of something we shouldn't name yet. Then Rhea called out from a distance, breaking it. Reality resumed its schedule.

That night, back at the hotel, Priya whispered, "Ma'am, are you sure you hate him?"
"Yes," I said too quickly.
She grinned. "Okay. Just checking. Because he looks at you like a cliff looks at the sky."

I didn't reply. But later, lying awake, I thought about that. How some people enter your life like an argument you secretly enjoy losing.

The next morning, before we left for Goa, I found a post-it on my laptop. Hand-drawn doodle of a plane with a caption: "Next time, don't run. Let the wrong flight land first." No signature. No need. I folded it into my journal. Maybe we were both a little lost. Maybe that was the point.

The Goa Mess

There's something about Goa that makes people lose their sense of boundaries. Maybe it's the salt in the air. Maybe it's the illusion that consequences don't exist where the ocean does. For me, it started with an email titled "Team bonding activity... optional (but not really)".

Three weeks into the campaign, we'd already covered six cities, five flights, and one minor existential crisis.
Everyone was running on caffeine, adrenaline, and Arjun's relentless optimism.

When the Goa leg began, I was hoping for peace, beach, content, wrap-up, done. But apparently, Arjun's definition of work involved near-death experiences disguised as fun.
"Cliff diving?" I repeated, reading the itinerary he'd made.
"Adventure builds trust," he said cheerfully.
"Therapy does too," I replied. "And no one dies there."
He grinned. "Relax, Khanna. It's safe. Locals do it all the time."
"Yes, because they probably know how to swim!"
He looked me dead in the eye. "You don't?"
"Of course I do," I lied. Badly.

By noon, we were standing at a cliff that looked straight out of a cinematic montage, sunlight bouncing off turquoise

water, waves crashing below, everyone cheering like they were auditioning for a Pepsi ad. Rhea had her GoPro ready. Priya was screaming in excitement. The videographers were flying drones. And me? I was silently writing my obituary. Arjun stood beside me, shirt half unbuttoned, hair a mess, radiating main-character energy.
"You're shaking," he teased.
"I'm strategizing," I shot back.
"About gravity?"
"About your murder."

He laughed. Loud. Free. The kind of laugh that made everyone else smile without knowing why.
Then he looked at me, seriously for a second.
"Trust me," he said softly. "I won't let you fall."

I don't know if it was the way he said it or the way the wind caught his voice, but something in me cracked. Maybe it was exhaustion. Maybe attraction. Maybe both.
"Fine," I said. "Once. Then we're done."
He offered his hand. I hesitated. Then I took it. And we jumped. For a moment, there was nothing but wild, screaming air. Then cold, brutal, cleansing water. When I surfaced, gasping, he was right there, laughter bubbling out of him.
"You did it!"
"I hate you!"
"You love me a little."

I splashed him in the face. He laughed harder. And just like that, something shifted, the kind of shift you don't notice until it's irreversible.

That evening, the team decided to celebrate. Bonfire on the beach, fairy lights, cheap beer, bad music, the holy trinity of poor decisions. Arjun was strumming his guitar again, because apparently he'd made a blood pact with the instrument. Rhea was filming everyone dancing; Priya was already tipsy enough to start matchmaking.

"Come dance!" Arjun called out.
"I don't dance."
"Neither do I. That's what makes it fun."

Before I could protest, he pulled me to the sand. The sand was still warm from the day's sun. Someone had dragged a Bluetooth speaker near the fire; an old Bollywood song crackled through the wind, something about moons and madness.

Arjun moved the way he did everything else without effort. Loose shirt, bare feet, hair damp from the sea. He wasn't even dancing as much as swaying, a rhythm that belonged to the ocean more than the song.

"Come on," he said, holding out a hand.
"No," I said automatically.

He tilted his head, the way he does when he knows he's already won.
"One song. If you hate it, I'll never ask again."

I sighed and stepped forward, because apparently resistance had a time limit around him.

At first, I stood stiffly, moving just enough to not look robotic.
He laughed. "You're thinking too much."
"I always think."
"Yeah, that's the problem."

He guided my hands, slow, patient. The air smelled of salt and fire and something reckless. When he twirled me, I tripped on the sand and crashed into him. His hands caught my waist before gravity could finish the joke.

The world went quiet for a second, just waves, music, and his breath against my cheek. My heart wasn't beating normally anymore; it was auditioning for a drum solo.
"See?" he whispered. "Falling isn't so bad."
I looked up at him, ready with some sarcastic comeback, but then a sudden, loud fireworks went off above us. And in that flicker of gold and red light, he kissed me. It wasn't planned. It wasn't gentle either. It was raw which felt like a question you don't want answered.

He tasted like salt and beer and trouble. My fingers found his shirt; his hand moved up to my neck; the noise of the party blurred into nothing. And then it hit me, the realization, the panic, the old instinct to run. I pulled away, breathless.

"Arjun..."

He looked at me, confused, hopeful, still too close.

"This shouldn't have happened," I said, stepping back.

"Because?"

"Because it complicates everything."

He smiled faintly. "Maybe simple was overrated."

I shook my head. "You don't understand. I have rules."

"I noticed. You follow them like religion."

"Exactly. And this..." I gestured vaguely between us, "...this breaks them."

He didn't argue. Just nodded, eyes softer than I'd ever seen.

"Okay. But rules don't stop gravity either."

I left before he could say anything else. The sound of fireworks followed me down the beach, their brightness and relentlessness almost mocking.

Back in my hotel room, I stared at my reflection. Sand in my hair. Mascara smudged. Lips still tingling. I hated that it felt right before it felt wrong. I hated that he didn't chase me. Mostly, I hated that a part of me wished he had.

The next morning, I was all business again with my laptop open, eyes cold, voice steady. He walked in for the debrief like nothing had happened.
"Morning, Ms Khanna," he said, in a perfectly polite.
"Morning, Mr Mehta," I replied.

Our team had no clue what had cracked the air between us. But every time our eyes met across the table, something unspoken hummed, a memory neither of us dared to touch.

Ghosting Season

The morning after Goa smelled like salt and regret. The ocean outside my hotel balcony looked too calm for the chaos in my head. People on the beach laughed, kids chased waves, someone played a badly tuned guitar. Meanwhile, I sat there wondering how to un-kiss a person who'd felt like déjà vu and disaster rolled into one. I'd spent years building rules. Never mix work and feelings. Never blur lines you'll have to redraw later. Never fall for the man who thinks spontaneity is a life philosophy. But Arjun had this way of making rules sound optional.

When the campaign wrapped, I did what I do best.. compartmentalize.
Emails. Check.
Deliverables. Check.
Heart. Under lock and password.
He said goodbye like it was just another airport moment. "Safe flight, Ms Khanna." "Always," I'd replied, and walked away without looking back. I told myself it was closure. But closure is just a prettier word for avoidance.

Back in Mumbai, the city welcomed me like an over-caffeinated ex, loud, demanding, impossible to ignore. I threw myself into work. Late nights. Client decks. A promotion rumoured to be around the corner. Everything I'd ever said I wanted was finally within reach. Except peace.

A week later, my phone buzzed during a meeting. Arjun Mehta tagged you in a post. My stomach did a full somersault. The video opened with a montage: hills, highways, laughter, and locals.
Voice-over:
"Sometimes, being lost is the only way to find what matters."
Hashtag: #InTransit.
The caption read:
"For everyone who's still figuring it out."

It was brilliant. Simple. Painful. The reel hit a million views in a day. Comments flooded in: "Life-changing." "He gets it." "This made me cry." I wanted to hate it. I couldn't. Because I knew exactly where that line came from. A road, a night, a woman who'd whispered she didn't know how to stay still.

That evening, Priya walked into my cabin waving her phone.
"Have you seen this campaign? Everyone's talking about it. They say the concept came from a heartbreak story."
I smiled tightly. "Good for them."
"You okay?" she asked.
"Of course. Why wouldn't I be?"

She looked unconvinced but didn't push. When she left, I replayed the reel again. And again. As if repetition could turn curiosity into closure.

The thing about ghosting is, it doesn't feel like disappearing. It feels like self-preservation, until you realize you're haunting yourself instead.

Every morning, I told myself I wouldn't check his page. Every night, I did. I told myself it was "professional curiosity." Because technically, he was my client. Technically, I was allowed to "stay updated on campaign performance." Except professionals don't zoom in on smiles or pause at three seconds to rewatch the way someone looks into the camera like he's still talking to them.

His new life was everywhere. Magazine interviews. Podcasts. Reposts of his campaign under #InTransit.
A Forbes feature titled "Meet the Man Redefining Modern Travel." The same man who'd once tripped over a suitcase and spilled chai on my presentation file. Now the internet worshipped him like a lifestyle guru. He posted from airports and mountains, wrote long captions about "trusting the detour," smiled like heartbreak was good PR. And I... I wrote a brand copy for toothpaste.

One night, at 2 a.m., Aisha texted me: "Still pretending you're over him?" I stared at the message for a long time.

Then replied: "He's doing fine. I'm proud of him." She wrote back instantly. "You don't sound proud. You sound possessed." She wasn't wrong. Because pride doesn't make your heart ache when you hear his voice in a thirty-second reel.

Possession does.

Meanwhile, Arjun was becoming a phenomenon. In one video, he stood on a cliff somewhere in Himachal, wind in his hair, voice steady. "You can't plan wonder. It finds you when you finally stop planning." In another, he was laughing with locals, helping build a homestay. "We're all in transit," the caption said. "Some people just make it look like home." And there it was again... that word.

Home.

The one thing I couldn't build with Excel sheets and brand decks.

At work, I got my promotion. New title, new clients, new corner cabin with a view of the skyline. People congratulated me, posted LinkedIn quotes about "hard work paying off." I smiled through it all. But every time my phone buzzed with another In Transit notification, it felt like someone whispering, This wasn't supposed to end here.

Weeks turned into months. I stopped posting. Stopped replying to friends. Stopped looking at travel brochures because everything reminded me of him. I wasn't jealous of his success. I was jealous of his peace. He'd turned our story into art. I'd turned mine into avoidance.

One night, after another client's dinner, I came home exhausted and scrolled without thinking. There he was.. new reel. Same smile. Same background music I'd once heard him hum under his breath in a candlelit dhaba. This time, the caption read: "To the girl who taught me that control isn't peace. I hope you found both." I froze. The room went quiet. Even the city outside seemed to hold its breath. I stared at the screen until the autoplay looped. Once. Twice. Thrice. And for the first time in months, I let myself cry, messy, tired, silent that tastes like salt and honesty.

When the tears stopped, I whispered to no one,
"You win, Arjun Mehta."
But somewhere deep down, I knew it wasn't a competition anymore. It was a calling. Maybe we were still in transit. Just on different roads.

Reunions & Rishtas

If life were a movie, this would be the part where violins start playing right before everything goes downhill, gracefully, of course. Because nothing says "moving on" like accidentally meeting your almost-lover at your best friend's wedding.

Aisha's engagement was supposed to be a happy distraction. She'd been dating Kabir (yes, our Kabir, the human embodiment of soft smiles and punctuality) for two years, and now they were finally making it official.

Destination wedding in Udaipur.
Three days.
Full Bollywood production.
I'd been hired to handle the digital event marketing because apparently, I couldn't just attend weddings anymore; I had to monetize them.

The palace looked like it had stepped straight out of a Sanjay Leela Bhansali fever dream: marble corridors, rose petals everywhere, fairy lights hanging like constellations. I arrived two days early with my laptop, my camera team, and a mild anxiety attack.
Aisha hugged me tight. "You look thinner!"
"That's called depression," I said sweetly.

She laughed. "Good. It photographs well."
She was glowing obnoxiously happy, in-love glow. I was genuinely happy for her, just also slightly allergic to joy that was sincere.

By the second day, the palace was buzzing. Families, friends, sangeet rehearsals, gossip networks forming like satellites. And then someone mentioned the performer. "A live band from Delhi," the planner said. "The lead singer's apparently gone viral recently. Some 'In Transit' thing?" I froze mid-sip. Of course. Of course the universe had booked him for entertainment.

That evening, during the mehendi, the guests gathered near the pool. Lanterns floating, laughter echoing, Aisha's cousins trying to outdo each other in reels. And then I heard it. That voice. Deep, steady, familiar in a way I could never mistake.

"Sometimes, we find our way back... not because we planned to, but because something in us forgot how to stay away."

He walked onto the stage, guitar in hand, spotlight catching the edge of his grin.
Arjun Mehta.
Hair longer. Beard scruffier. Eyes still capable of emotional damage. Our eyes met for half a second. And everything I'd

buried came crashing back the Goa night, the cliff jump, the words I'd run from. I looked away first.

After the performance, everyone crowded around him for selfies, compliments, and quick chats. He took it all in stride, effortlessly charming. I told myself I wasn't watching. But of course I was.

Later, as I escaped to the back garden to breathe, a familiar voice said, "Still allergic to crowds?" I turned. Vihaan stood there, our old college friend, the one who'd once lent me notes and now worked in Singapore. He looked the same, clean-cut with kind eyes and that steady energy that makes you feel safe even when you don't want to. We hugged.
"You look exactly like you did in college," he said.
"Thanks. That's what burnout does, preserves you like time froze."
He laughed. "Still dramatic."
"Still honest," I shot back.

We walked by the lake, catching up on everything and nothing. He told me he was finally considering moving back to India. I told him I was still working too much and feeling too little. Somewhere in the distance, Arjun's voice floated from the speakers, testing sound for the sangeet 123 check check. Vihaan noticed my silence. "You okay?" "Yeah," I lied.

The next day, during sangeet rehearsals, fate decided to flex again. Aisha had paired me with Arjun for a dance number. "Great chemistry!" she said, clapping her hands. "Terrible idea," I muttered. He stood across the room, smirking already in place. "So, partners again," he said. "Involuntarily," I replied. We started rehearsing. Or, more accurately, arguing disguised as choreography.

"You're off-beat."

"I'm improvising."

"You're supposed to twirl me, not trip me!"

"Maybe you should let go once in a while."

He caught my wrist mid-spin, and for a heartbeat, everything stilled. The music, the laughter, the noise. It was just the two of us, breath close to breath, eyes locked in that risky nostalgia.

I pulled away. "This isn't a movie."

He smiled softly. "No. But it could've been."

By the time the sangeet started, the palace had turned into a dream sequence. Strings of marigold hung like sunlight, the lake reflected fireworks, and someone somewhere was rehearsing lines that sounded like a declaration of love.

I kept myself busy behind my laptop checking schedules, fixing lighting cues, pretending to be indispensable. Anything to avoid the man with the microphone.

When Arjun finally walked on stage, the crowd erupted. He belonged there, confident, alive, magnetic. He sang a new version of Ilahi, slower, rougher, as if every word had walked barefoot through memory. People swayed, couples held hands. I looked everywhere except at him. But mid-song, he said into the mic, "This one's for the people who run when it gets real. May you find your way back someday." The audience cheered. I froze. I could feel his gaze even through the lights. And for a second, I wondered if he'd just confessed in front of two hundred strangers.

After the performance, Aisha pulled me onto the dance floor. "Stop hiding, Naina! You used to love dancing." "I used to love many bad ideas," I said. And then Vihaan appeared, extending his hand. "Come on. No escape this time." He was safe, predictable, and kind. He spun me slowly, and for a moment, I let the music drown the noise in my head. But then I noticed Arjun watching us from the bar. His expression was unreadable, a glass in his hand, and a smile that felt too polite to be real.

Later, when the crowd thinned and the music softened into background hum, I stepped outside to the terrace. The lake was quiet. So was I. I didn't hear him approach until he spoke. "You dance with everyone but me." I turned. He was standing in the doorway, sleeves rolled, voice steady but eyes stormy.
"This isn't the time or place, Arjun."

"Then when? You've been avoiding me for months."
"I had work. Life. Priorities."
"Right," he said softly. "And none of them had space for honesty?"

The words landed harder than I expected. He took a step closer. "You kissed me like you meant it, Naina. And then you vanished like it was a crime." I swallowed. "Because it felt like one." He exhaled, shaking his head. "You keep calling everything that scares you a mistake. One day you'll run out of things worth feeling." For a moment, neither of us spoke. The only sound was the ripple of water and our hearts doing what logic couldn't fix. Then Vihaan's voice called from behind, "Naina, everyone's looking for you!" He stopped when he saw us. The air thickened. Arjun looked away first. "Of course," he said quietly. "Perfect timing, as always." And he walked back inside.

Vihaan frowned. "Did I interrupt something?"
"No," I lied again. "You saved me."
He hesitated, then said, "Good. Because I was actually hoping to talk to you."
We sat by the balustrade, moonlight slicing through the silence. "I know this might sound sudden," he began, "but I've always liked you, Naina. I thought maybe... now that we're both older, wiser..."
I stared at the water. Something twisted inside me, not guilt, or excitement, just confusion.

"Vihaan, you're wonderful," I said gently. "But I'm not sure I'm ready for..."

He smiled faintly. "I figured you'd say that. I just needed you to know."

He stood, brushed the dust off his trousers, and added, "But whoever he is... he's lucky. You still look at him like he's home."

That night, I lay in bed staring at the ceiling, wedding songs echoing faintly through the corridors.

Two men.

One safe.

One storm.

And me... somewhere between nostalgia and fear. Outside, fireworks burst over the palace. Inside, my heart whispered, Not again. But another voice, quieter, replied, Maybe once more.

The Shaadi Circus

If therapy ever feels too expensive, attend an Indian wedding. One day of haldi, mehendi, or sangeet will teach you more about family trauma, unresolved exes, and suppressed feelings than a year of counseling ever could.

By the second morning in Udaipur, the palace had officially turned into chaos with choreography. Aunties in matching yellow yelling about missing flower petals. Groomsmen half-drunk before breakfast. Cousins filming "behind-the-scenes" content like this was a reality show. And me... trying to keep everything under control with a clipboard, an espresso, and zero emotional stability.

Aisha's haldi started late, obviously. Kabir's cousins arrived two hours behind schedule but somehow still found time to start a flash mob. My camera team was losing their minds. And then there was him. Arjun Mehta. Dressed in an off-white kurta, sleeves rolled, skin sunlit, smile mildly dangerous. Performing again because apparently, weddings and heartbreak had become his natural habitat.

I was pretending to check guest lists when I saw him talking to some girl near the marigold archway. Pretty. Loud laugh. The kind of confidence that looks like perfume. He leaned in as she said something; she touched his arm lightly. He laughed too freely. It shouldn't have bothered me. It did. I told myself to focus on the haldi playlist. Except now I was scrolling through the songs like I was personally curating the soundtrack to my jealousy.

He noticed me watching. Of course he did. And like the drama queen the universe trained him to be, he turned up the charm. Offered her juice, whispered something, laughed louder.

I bit my lip and muttered to Priya, "Unbelievable."

"What happened, ma'am?"

"Nothing. The sun's just... aggressive today."

Right. The sun.

When we crossed paths near the haldi stage, he smirked.

"Careful, Khanna. You're glaring at people again."

"Just exercising my eyes," I said sweetly.

"Intense workout."

I exhaled through my nose. "You can't even commit to a playlist, forget a person."

The words escaped before my brain could censor them. He froze for half a second, then smiled—slow, knowing, dangerous.

"At least I don't commit to the wrong ones."

Mic. Drop. Even the dhol seemed to pause for dramatic effect. I walked away, pretending I didn't care. I did. Every time he passed by, every stolen glance across the courtyard, every forced smile during photo ops, it all added up like static electricity. The more I avoided him, the louder the tension hummed between us.

By afternoon, the sky turned moody. Dark clouds gathered above the palace like the universe had decided we deserved a rain sequence. And then, as if on cue, it started pouring. Of course, instead of running for cover, the guests started cheering. Because in every Indian wedding, rain isn't an inconvenience, it's divine approval.

Someone turned up the music. People danced barefoot on marble floors, soaked and laughing. It was madness. It was magic. The rain arrived like it had been waiting for its cue. Within minutes, haldi paste was running down arms, flowers drooped, and the courtyard transformed into a glittering mess of laughter and puddles.

Aisha squealed, dragging Kabir into the downpour.
Someone shouted, "Rain dance!" and the DJ, clearly a man of culture, switched to "Sadda Haq."

I tried to escape to the verandah, clutching my phone like it was an umbrella of dignity. But Priya shoved me back. "Come on, ma'am! You'll regret not dancing when you're eighty!" I already regretted many things. What was one more?

Arjun was in the middle of it all, shirt plastered to his skin, hands lifted to the sky. Completely alive. Completely infuriating. He saw me standing on the edge and gestured. "Come on, Khanna!" I shook my head. He splashed water in my direction. I glared. He smirked. And that was that. I stepped forward. Cold water hit my face, laughter broke out around us, and for the first time in months, I stopped thinking.

We danced. It was messy, soaked, ridiculous where everyone loses rhythm and finds freedom instead. Someone twirled me, someone else threw flower petals, and through it all, Arjun kept orbiting closer. A sudden thunderclap made me jump. He caught my hand on instinct, fingers slipping but not letting go.
Our eyes met. Everything else disappeared.

Rain drummed between us, turning seconds into slow motion. He was still holding my hand. I should've pulled away. I didn't. He smiled softly this time, not the teasing one, but the kind that knows too much.
"Still scared of falling?" he asked quietly. I breathed out, "Still pretending it's fun?"
Lightning flashed.
Somewhere behind us, people cheered as Aisha and Kabir kissed under an umbrella. But we... We just stood there, caught between denial and déjà vu. He leaned closer, voice low.

"You know what's funny?"
"What?"
"You look happiest when you stop fighting me."
I laughed, half-choked, half-sincere. "Don't flatter yourself."
He grinned. "Too late."

And then the music changed to something slower, older, heartbreakingly romantic. Tum Se Hi filtered through the speakers like nostalgia had been waiting its turn. He took a step closer. I didn't move back. For a heartbeat, it felt like the world had narrowed to raindrops and heartbeats. If this were a movie, this would've been the second-chance kiss. But real life likes cliff-hangers. Someone yelled my name. Reality returned, breathless. I pulled my hand free.
"Don't read into it," I said.
He smiled almost sadly this time.
"Too late for that too."

Later that night, I sat by my window, wrapped in a towel, hair dripping on my notebook. Outside, the rain hadn't stopped. Inside, neither had the noise in my head. I replayed every glance, every word, every almost. I told myself it was nothing. But my heart, traitor that it is, whispered, Then why does it feel like everything?

The Flight That Never Took Off

Weddings end the way movies do, music fades, the confetti falls, and everyone pretends nothing's changed, even though deep down they know it has. After three days of haldi, sangeet, and rain-drenched chaos, Aisha's shaadi finally wound down. The guests were leaving. The decorators were half-asleep. And I was packing my bags like running away was part of my itinerary.

London was waiting. The interview I'd dreamed about since college, with the creative director at a global travel firm. It was everything I'd worked for, everything I thought I wanted. So why did it feel like betrayal?

Arjun was nowhere near the lobby when I came down with my suitcase. Good. Good was safer. Except, of course, he appeared the moment I called for a cab. White shirt. Sleeves rolled. That same maddening calm that made silence feel like a conversation.

"You're leaving already?"

"Some of us have jobs," I said.

"Some of us have hearts," he replied lightly, but the joke landed heavily.

I sighed. "Don't do this, Arjun."

"Do what?"

"Make me feel like I'm walking away from something I don't even understand."

He really looked at me then, "You understand it. You just don't trust it."

The driver loaded my bags. The palace behind us shimmered in the morning light, quiet now, like it had seen too much. I tried to keep it professional.

"Take care of yourself. The campaign, your work, it's beautiful. I really mean that."

He nodded. "And you. You'll do great in London."

"Yeah," I whispered. "I will."

The lie stung both of us.

He stepped closer. For a moment, it felt like the rain all over again. But instead of closing the distance, he said softly, "Go. Miss your flight if you have to. But don't miss your life."

Airports are terrible places for good-byes. They turn every decision into a security check. You walk in certain of your destination and walk out wondering what you've left behind.

The cab ride to Udaipur airport was silent except for the sound of rain tapping against the windows. I kept staring at the blur of the city, trying to convince myself that this was the right choice. Better jobs. Bigger dreams. A clean slate that didn't smell like him.

When I reached the terminal, the glass doors slid open and that familiar airport chill hit me, the same one from the day we'd met. A full-circle joke the universe clearly found funny.

While I queued at check-in, my phone buzzed.
A message from Aisha:
He didn't stay for breakfast. Said he had an early shoot. You okay?
I typed back:
Perfect.
Then deleted it.
Because perfection had never been my truth.

Half an hour away, somewhere on the road out of Udaipur, Arjun's car crawled through the drizzle. He kept the radio off. The windshield wipers moved in rhythm, a metronome for the thoughts he wasn't ready to admit. He should've said something real. He should've stopped her. But loving someone like Naina meant respecting the fences she built even if they shut him out. He drove past the lake where lanterns still floated from last night's ceremony. One of them flickered, hesitated, then stayed lit. It was ridiculous how much hope could fit into a single light.

Back at the airport, the announcement echoed: "Flight 9W-204 to London boarding shortly." I moved toward the gate, heartbeat steady, hands trembling. Every step forward felt like betrayal disguised as ambition. I glanced at my phone again. No message. No reason to stay. And yet... When they called final boarding, I didn't move. The attendant looked at me. "Ma'am?" I smiled, a little too calmly. "Could you please cancel my seat?"

Outside, the rain had softened to mist. I stood by the taxi stand, suitcase beside me, heart finally quiet. Somewhere far away, a car pulled over near a phone tower. Arjun stepped out, tilted his head up, and let the rain fall over his face. Different skies. Same ache. A song played faintly from a roadside café

"If you never miss your flight, maybe you never arrive."

He laughed under his breath, the laugh that still somehow hurt. And for the first time, neither of us knew whether the story was ending or just turning into something else.

In Transit

They call it a comeback when you win something you once lost. But sometimes, it's just peace disguised as applause.

Six months later, I was standing on a stage in Mumbai, lights too bright, heart too loud. Our agency's travel campaign had just won Best Digital Film of the Year. I should've been thrilled. I was somewhere beneath the disbelief. The host handed me the mic. "Tell us about the story behind this film," he said.
Story.
Right.
Where did one even start?

I took a breath. "It began with a mistake," I said. The crowd burst into laughter. They thought I was being witty. I wasn't. On the screen behind me, the opening clip rolled, the viral one. The wrong flight. The roadside dhaba. Me yelling at a man holding a guitar.

The hall erupted in laughter again. And just like that, it all came rushing back: the chai steam, the monsoon light, the me who still believed control was safe.

Somewhere near the back row, flashes from cameras blinked like memories. I kept speaking, voice steadier now. "This video... It reminded me that the best journeys aren't the ones we plan. They're the ones that ruin our plans completely."

Applause.
But it sounded distant, muffled by the weight behind my ribs.

When the clip ended, I froze for a heartbeat. Because in the last frame before the logo faded there he was.
Arjun, laughing into the camera, sunlight on his face, saying, "Trust the detour."

The audience laughed softly. I blinked a few times, hoping the tears wouldn't win this time. The applause faded, replaced by that odd ringing silence that follows a standing ovation. It was the kind of silence that lets you hear your own heartbeat, your own truth. I smiled for the cameras, waved at the audience, and said my thank-yous. Outside, my colleagues celebrated. Inside, I was somewhere else entirely. Because success feels different when the person who taught you to dream isn't there to see it.

Backstage smelled of flowers and old makeup. The award was heavier than it looked. Everyone kept hugging me, telling me I deserved it. Maybe I did. Maybe I didn't. I slipped away quietly to the balcony, needing air that wasn't full of congratulations.

Mumbai shimmered below, neon and noise, the kind of city that never sleeps and never apologises. I leaned against the railing and let the wind hit my face. Half a year of work, wins, interviews and yet I still felt in transit.

A voice broke through behind me. "Nice speech, Ms. Khanna." I turned. And there he was. Arjun. Standing in the doorway like he'd just stepped out of a memory. Same eyes, same calm, slightly shorter hair, but a softer, steadier energy. "How did you..." I began. He lifted his phone, smiling. "Got invited. They said one of my old videos was being screened. Thought I'd come see who stole my line." I laughed through the lump in my throat. "You trademarked detours now?" "Only the emotional kind." We stood there, silence stretching between us like a familiar road.

He nodded toward the award in my hand.
"Looks good on you."
"So does peace," I said quietly.
He smiled. "Finally found some."
"Where?"
"In between places. Where I stop pretending I'm over people I'm not."

The honesty caught me off guard. It always did with him. I swallowed. "I missed my flight that day."

"I know," he said quietly. "I waited at the airport until the last announcement. Figured if the plane left and you didn't, it meant something."
"It did," I whispered.
After a pause, the question slipped out before I could stop it. "If you were there... if you knew I stayed back... why didn't you come find me?" He looked at me for a long moment, eyes heavy with something between regret and holding back. "Because you looked like someone who'd finally chosen herself," he said softly. "And I didn't want to walk in and make it about me again." I blinked, stunned.

He gave a faint smile. "You were always running to fix everything, Naina.. your plans, people, the world. That night, you finally stood still. And I... I didn't want to be the reason you moved again." The silence that followed didn't feel awkward. It felt full. Like closure, finally learning how to breathe.

The city lights flickered below us, like tiny affirmations. He stepped closer. Not too close. Just enough. "So," he said softly, "where to next, Ms. Planner?" I smiled, tears threatening but not winning.
"Wherever life forgets to warn me."
He laughed, shaking his head. "Finally speaking my language."

Somewhere in the hall, a new song started—something slow, hopeful, unmistakably filmy. I looked at him, eyes still wet. "Still scared of falling?" he asked. I took a breath. "Maybe this time, I'll jump first." And for the first time since everything fell apart, it didn't feel like a detour. It felt like an arrival.

The Universe Rearranges

There's a moment between endings and beginnings that feels like standing at a station while every train leaves except yours. Silence, movement, choice.

After the awards night, life moved faster than my heart could follow. Emails from London piled up, contracts, accommodation options, an official "Congratulations, we can't wait to have you on board." Everyone said I'd made it. But every time I read the offer letter, something inside me whispered, Made it where?

A week later, I was at my desk in Mumbai, surrounded by half-packed boxes. Outside, the city buzzed like it was trying to be my soundtrack. On the screen, my resignation letter blinked back at me.

The cursor was steady. My decision wasn't. I stared at it until sunrise. Then I hit send. It didn't feel like failure. It felt like finally letting go of something that was never really mine.

A few days later, I met Reva, Arjun's sister, at a café in Bandra. I'd met Reva once before, months ago, back when Arjun and I were still somewhere between friends and almost. He'd dragged me to this open mic night in Andheri, promising "no small talk, just music." I'd expected a typical dimly lit pub with off-key singers. What I didn't expect was Reva, his younger sister walking up on stage with a ukulele and the confidence of someone who'd never known stage fright.

She'd dedicated her song "to all the overthinkers pretending to be chill." Arjun had laughed beside me and whispered, "She's talking about you." And I'd rolled my eyes, pretending not to smile. After her set, she hugged me like we'd known each other forever.

That's how Reva was instant warmth, unfiltered chaos, no introduction required. She'd insisted we follow each other on Instagram that very night. And though we never really stayed in touch, she'd occasionally reply to my stories with things like "you look dangerously happy, is he the reason?"

So when her text popped up out of nowhere now "You probably won't reply, but I'm in Bandra. Coffee?" I couldn't pretend it didn't pull at something old and unfinished.

The café was crowded, noisy, and lively in Bandra on a weekend. I found a corner table by the window and tried to look casual, though my heart was pacing like it knew something I didn't. Reva walked in like a storm, curls, laughter, bangles, and that familiar "I'm late but I bring chaos" energy. She waved, spotted me, and half-ran across the café.

"Look at you!" she said, hugging me tight. "Still drinking cold coffee in winter? Iconic."
I laughed. "You look exactly the same."
"Please," she said, flipping her hair. "Therapy, serums, and Himalayan air. I'm practically a new woman."

We ordered cutting chai and fries, slipping into small talk the way people do when they're trying not to talk about what actually matters. Work, Mumbai traffic, the same old dance. Then, in between bites of fries, she looked up and said,
"So… are we pretending we're not going to talk about him, or should I just start?"
I sighed. "Reva.."
She smirked. "Relax. I'm not here to play cupid. Just… consider me the postman. With gossip."

She stirred her chai dramatically.
"He's in Himachal."
I blinked. "Doing what?"
"Running a music café. Started as a pop-up for trekkers, now it's this whole thing. Live sessions, jam nights, stray dogs, bad coffee. Classic Arjun turning wanderlust into a lifestyle."
I smiled faintly. "Of course."
Reva tilted her head. "He doesn't talk about you, you know. But he talks around you. All the time."
I frowned. "What does that even mean?"

She leaned closer, lowering her voice.
"Like when he says, 'I miss the city when it rains', or 'some silences sound familiar.' You're in every sentence, just without your name."

Silence stretched between us. I stared out the window at the street below, watching strangers hurry through the drizzle. Reva smiled gently. "He told me not to tell you anything. So obviously, here we are."
I laughed, "Still defying him, huh?"
"Always," she said, grinning. "He's my favourite person to annoy."
Then she reached for her bag and stood. "Anyway, I've delivered the message. What you do with it is up to you."
Before I could respond, she leaned down and added softly,
"Just... don't wait for perfect timing, Naina. It doesn't exist. Sometimes you've got to miss the right flight twice before you realise it's the only one that matters."

And with that, she left with curls bouncing, leaving the faint scent of jasmine and mischief behind. I sat there long after she was gone, stirring a cup of cold chai. Outside, the city was noisy and alive, but inside, everything had gone quiet. Maybe the universe had stopped waiting for me to figure it out. Maybe it had started rearranging things already.

That night I opened a map. Not Google because apparently I still like paper cuts and getting lost the old fashioned way.

Folded, frayed, the kind you can trace with your fingers. Himachal looked impossibly far and strangely near. I drew a circle around it and whispered, “Okay, universe. Your move.”

The next morning, I bought a one-way bus ticket. Not a flight. No shortcuts this time. The bus station smelled of rain and chai. Dozens of engines coughed awake, people shouting goodbyes over the hiss of tyres. I should have felt nervous, but there was something grounding about not rushing for once. The last time I'd travelled like this, I was running from something. This time, I was moving toward it.

I found a seat by the window. Old Bollywood songs were playing on the driver's radio, crackly and full of hope, somehow familiar. When the bus pulled out of the terminal, Mumbai shrank behind a blur of monsoon grey, and the road stretched ahead like a promise.

For hours, I watched landscapes change the way moods do, cities turning into fields, fields dissolving into fog. People came and went at each stop; conversations rose and disappeared like passing waves.

A little boy across the aisle offered me a biscuit. His mother smiled, “First time in the hills?” I nodded. “Then you'll come back changed,” she said, as if it were a fact of geography. I believed her.

By dawn, the air grew thinner, cooler. Pine trees lined the curves, the sky the pale blue of beginnings. I opened the window wider and let the wind mess my hair, my thoughts. Somewhere between half-sleep and memory, I imagined him.. his easy laugh, his smile, the way he looked at sunsets like they were answers.For the first time, thinking about Arjun didn't hurt. It felt like finally exhaling.

At a roadside halt, the driver shouted, "Chai break!" I stepped out into the chill. Steam rose from paper cups, and the first sunlight spilled over the mountains. Everything smelled of earth after rain. It hit me then, how all this time, I'd been chasing destinations when the journey itself had been quietly rearranging me.

Back on the bus, I opened my journal and wrote,

———

"Maybe the universe doesn't take things away.
It just shifts them until you're ready to see them differently."

———

For the first time in a long while, that sentence didn't feel like homework.
It felt true.

As the road climbed higher, a small wooden sign appeared on the hillside:
"The Transit Café – Live Music, Open Hearts."

I smiled before I even knew why. The driver honked twice and said, “Madam, this is your stop.” I stepped off the bus, heart steady, sky wide, wind singing through the pines. Not for closure. For clarity.

The Right Detour

The road curved one last time before revealing a small wooden café tucked between two pine-covered slopes.
A hand-painted sign read: The Transit Café – Live Music, Open Hearts. The same name I'd written in my notebook months ago. Maybe the universe really did eavesdrop when we weren't careful.

Wind carried the faint strum of a guitar. Inside, travellers sat wrapped in shawls, mugs of steaming coffee between their hands. Candles flickered on every table, rain drumming softly on the tin roof. And there he was. Arjun. On a small stage lit by fairy lights, singing something half-forgotten, half-familiar. His eyes were closed, voice low, the kind of sound that finds you before you realise you were listening. He looked... peaceful. No spotlight, no chaos, just a man in rhythm with his own heartbeat.

I stood at the doorway, rain dripping from my hair, my shoes squeaking on the wooden floor. Someone looked my way, smiled, and nudged the person next to them. He opened his eyes. Saw me. The music faltered for half a breath. Then he smiled. The crowd watched curiously like they were waiting for something. I walked closer, heart hammering, every step an unfinished sentence. He lifted the mic, half-laughing. “Looks like someone missed another flight.”

I took it from him before I lost my nerve. Rain roared louder, like the universe turning up the volume.
“I took the wrong flight again,” I said into the mic, voice trembling but steady enough. Then smiled. “But maybe this time… it’s the right one.”

The café erupted in applause, a few whistles, and a shout of “Say yes already!” We laughed and that sounded like relief. He set his guitar down, stepped forward. For once, neither of us hesitated. Rain, music, laughter… everything blurred into one long-awaited moment as his hands found mine and the world finally felt aligned. Up close, he still smelled like rain and coffee. “Long way to come for an encore,” he murmured. “Some songs deserve a second verse,” I said.

For a moment, neither of us moved. It felt like the world had paused, leaving us stuck between laughter and lightning. Then he pulled me in slowly, carefully, as if testing if the world would hold its breath for us again. It did. The kiss wasn’t fireworks this time. It was like endless rain. A quiet homecoming that felt like a new start.

When we finally broke apart, he whispered against my forehead,
“I kept the café name for you, you know.”

"Because of our campaign?"
"Because of what it meant.
In transit... between fear and faith, logic and love.. you still found me."
I laughed softly. "I was just following bad directions."
He grinned. "Exactly."

The café crowd cheered when he picked up the guitar. He motioned to the mic. "Stay," he said. "Sing something with me." I shook my head. "You know I can't sing." "Neither can I. That's why it works." So I stayed. We hummed through an old tune, off-key but happy, and for once I didn't care how it sounded. The world outside poured and shimmered, and inside, everything felt like it had landed exactly where it was supposed to.

Weeks later, I started helping him run the café. We served travellers, painted walls, and hosted open mics. Every night, music spilled into the mountains, and somewhere between refilling cups and rewriting dreams, I realised home had never been a place. It had always been a person who didn't flinch when I arrived unannounced.

One evening, as the sun sank behind the peaks, Arjun handed me a new signboard. Fresh paint, uneven letters, his handwriting. It read: *"The Right Detour."* He smiled. "Felt like a promotion." I smiled back. "Felt like destiny finally learning directions."

Outside, buses rumbled down the hill. Inside, laughter echoed. He reached for my hand. And as the first drops of rain began again, I thought of that day years ago.. the wrong flight, the chaos, the beginning disguised as a mistake.

Some love stories aren't planned.
They just miss a flight...
and find their way home.

Epilogue - Dil in Transit

I never planned to post it. It was supposed to be a personal vlog, something just for me, like a scrapbook for the soul. But one evening, while the mountains yawned into twilight and Arjun was tuning his guitar for the café crowd, I set my camera on the windowsill and hit record.

The frame caught the fairy lights, the half-empty mugs, the view that never got old.
"Hi," I said to the lens.
"It's been a while.

This isn't a travel video. This is... what happens after the trip ends. When the tickets are used, the memories are edited, and you're still figuring out where 'home' starts." I paused, watching the light fade.

"People think love is a destination," I went on. "Like a city you book in advance. But sometimes it's a detour.. a wrong flight, a chai stop, a stranger who makes the noise in your head finally quiet."

A laugh slipped out. "Sometimes it's a café at the edge of nowhere, and sometimes it's the courage to stay once you find it."

I looked straight into the lens then, heart soft, voice steady.
"I think I was always scared of missing flights,
until I realised the ones you miss on purpose
are the ones that save you."

I ended the video there, no music, no outro. Just rain beginning again on the roof. That night, I uploaded it anyway, titled it Dil in Transit.

By morning, the internet had found it. Comments poured in. Strangers wrote about the people they didn't chase, the journeys they did. It felt like all our detours had finally met online. Among the thousands of notifications, one stood out.

Arjun Mehta 💬:
"Still hate flights. Still love you."
I smiled, typing back before my heart could overthink it.
Naina Khanna 💬:
"Good. I'm driving."

The café doors opened, the mountains stretched awake, and somewhere in the valley below, a bus honked twice as if the universe was laughing with us.

A Small Note to My Readers

If you've reached this page, it means you've finished reading my book and that alone means the world to me. You took time out of your life to live inside these words, and I can't tell you how deeply that humbles me.

I have a small request for you, nothing fancy, just something from the heart.

If you haven't connected with me on social media yet, please do! I truly want to talk to you, hear your thoughts, your feelings, your favorite lines, everything you felt while reading this story.

■ Instagram: @author.simranbhandari
■ Email: official.simranbhandari@gmail.com
● Website: https://wordsbysimran.carrd.co

Please share your reviews wherever you can, on Amazon, on Instagram, with your friends, or even over a cup of chai. Tell people what this book made you feel, because your words are what help this story travel farther than I ever could.

You are the reason these pages mean something. With every post, every tag, every shared line, you give this book a new heartbeat.

In short... spread the word. Make some noise for your book, because now, this story doesn't belong to just me, it belongs to all of us.

And if you have a little more time, mail me personally or DM me and tell me what stayed with you:
Which chapter touched you most?
Who was your favorite character?
Did the ending feel like ?

I promise I will read every message. And I'll reply, because connection is the real reason I write.

Until the next book,
Keep reading, keep healing, keep loving and remember, you are never too late to start again.

With all my heart,
Yours truly,
Simran Bhandari ■

Acknowledgements

They say every story is born twice, once in the writer's mind, and once in the hearts of those who believe in it. This one would've never made it past the first page without the people who held my hand through every rewrite, every breakdown, every "what if I'm not good enough?" moment.

First, to my parents, for loving me through all my detours and for teaching me that strength and softness can coexist. You've been my constant compass, and every dream I chase has your fingerprints on it.

To my closest circle, the friends who became family thank you for being the laughter between drafts and the voices that told me to keep going when I wanted to quit. You know exactly who you are, and you know exactly how much I love you.

To the one who inspired pieces of this story, thank you for showing me that some meetings are meant to rearrange entire universes. You may not realise it, but every line I wrote about courage and chaos carries a little bit of you.

I'm endlessly grateful to my readers, for picking up this book, for seeing themselves in its imperfect, beautiful characters, and for trusting me to tell a story that feels like a film and a feeling all at once. You make the late nights and self-doubt worth it.

To my incredible team, my editor, my publisher, and every person who believed that a "wrong flight" could lead to the right kind of love, thank you for turning my messy drafts into magic.

And finally, to the universe, for every delay, every heartbreak, every "not yet" that became "right on time."
This story is my thank-you note to you.

About the Author

Simran Bhandari is a software engineer by profession and a storyteller by passion. Between lines of code and cups of chai, she found her way back to words, weaving stories about love, timing, and all the beautiful mess in between.

Her writing blends modern relationships with quiet moments of introspection, exploring what it means to love, lose, and find yourself again.

Dil in Transit is her debut novel, a heartfelt desi romcom about missed flights, found hearts, and the kind of love that arrives when you stop chasing it.

When she isn't writing, she can be found watching sunsets, collecting quotes, or turning everyday chaos into stories.

Follow her journey on Instagram @author.simranbhandari.

www.ingramcontent.com/pod-product-compliance
Lightning Source LLC
Chambersburg PA
CBHW022201160726
48282CB00024B/272
9789334442151